silence

and

sorrow

BIRD

Ever wonder what it would feel like to give in to your dark side?

To release your inner serial killer?

Well, this is me doing just that.

This one is for your dark side.

WARNINGS

Silence and Sorrow is a dark romance erotica novella.

This book is not recommended for persons under the age of eighteen.

This book contains multiple potential triggers that may be not be suitable for all readers. Caution is advised. Please read through the entire list of triggers and make the decision to continue or not continue on your own. xoxo

This book contains depictions of emotional abusive from a family member, murder, child abuse, kidnapping, torture, stabbing, and light blood play.

This is a work of pure fiction.

Enjoy, Little Bird.

KALIUS

ONE

I always underestimate how time-consuming cleaning up blood can be, especially the splatter that seems to find every nook and cranny of this room.

With only an hour before my dinner meeting, I need to finish my cleanup before I get ready. I could leave the mess, but it would annoy me, knowing that I'd have to do it when I returned, and I'm going to be annoyed enough as it is.

These meetings are always a poor excuse to spend company money at a fancy restaurant to cover details and updates that could easily be shared in an email. But I'll be nice and play the part, be the serious and caring CEO that I'm known to be, all while desperate to rip off that mask and return here, where I can let my real self out.

BIRD

After pressure-washing the floor with a bleach mixture, I squeegee the water toward the drain in the middle of the floor. Once the metallic scent of blood is replaced by the aroma of cleaning products, I take a quick shower in the en suite of my kill room and change into a fitted all-black suit, opting out of the choking tie.

"Ahh," I sigh from the satisfaction of my room being restored to its sparkling glory, although the look of the walls painted red in blood is gratifying in its own way.

Spritzing myself with cologne, I grab my phone and tuck it into the inside pocket of my coat. Picking up my other phone, the one that remains hidden from anyone but me, I check the notifications, feeling my spine tingle at the possibilities of what is to come. So many people to choose from, so many who deserve to die from the cruelty of my own two hands.

I'll never understand the brains of the people I target, although I believe the word *people* might be too human of a term. They are animals, inhuman monsters with no morals. They prey upon children with ease. I've considered if they were born this way, if some part of their DNA made them who they are, or if some tragedy or moment in their lives turned them into predators.

I've often wondered what made my brain so seemingly different from everyone else's. There wasn't a point in my life when my thoughts seemed to change; they just always were this way, darker than others, freer and .

more fearless.

I don't think inside a box. I'm not collared by society's standards. I think without boundaries and act accordingly

When I was a child, I had to learn the hard way that my thoughts and desires were something to be ashamed of, something to be kept hidden. I remember the very moment that I became aware of my *differences*.

I was four years old, playing with my mother's friend's children. The older sibling, Eli, had shoved his sister, Penelope, into the fridge really hard, and she began to cry.

So, I punished him.

I shoved him back hard enough that he broke his arm on the fall to the ground. I didn't know that was such a wrong thing to do. I'd just thought about it, and I'd acted. I couldn't understand why my parents were so angry with me or why I never saw Eli or Penelope again.

I learned many things that day from Eli, Penelope, my parents, and the world in general. Life isn't fair; it's warped and twisted. Eli hurt Penelope and had no consequences—at least any that would make a difference in his future actions. He just got away with it because the adults were hesitant to punish him the way he deserved.

The people who get ahead in life are ones who take what they want unapologetically. They are also the people who fit with the narrative, the ones that fit in the boring and plain straight-walled box of society. I wasn't born to fit in that box, but I have molded myself over the years to appear as if I always have.

This room is the only place where I can rip away all shreds of the facade and let my real self out to play, living thoughtlessly and without reserve, as I truly am.

A perfect soundproof room in the basement of my home has become my only peace of mind in this nasty world.

Day in and day out, I see the monsters that lurk in real life. Some disguised as doctors, or businessmen, or teachers, or even your loving family members. The type of monsters that prey on children and feel no remorse for the irreparable damage they inflict. All they can think of is themselves, and they bathe in it.

Sometime ago, I made it my mission to take as many down as I can. One by one, purging the world of its evil. I have successfully disposed of seventy-nine monsters, ones who were forced to lie in the bed they'd made. I find them by pretending to be an underage boy or girl. They reach out and message the profiles, unknowingly speaking to the person who is going to end their life.

Sometimes, I talk to them for a month or longer, or a day or two, or even mere minutes before the urges begin to become so loud in my mind that I have to act. I don't know if the phrase *killer tingle* would be an acceptable term, but it's what I've always called it in my mind.

SILENCE AND SORROW

A sensation that warms my spine, tingles the back of my neck, dries my mouth, and consumes me completely. Once it begins, it must be seen through to the end. I can't function, not truly, until its demands are met and blood is spilled.

Locking up my basement, I leave that side of me behind the closed door as I cross the marble foyer toward my front door.

I used to believe that something was wrong with me, that *I* was a monster. But I was wrong. I'm an avenging angel, condemning the real monstrosities of this world to a hell of my own creation.

I don't hate playing the part of CEO all the time. It can be fun occasionally. But tonight is not one of those nights.

I have always been smart, more intelligent than most. I have a master's degree in business and a bachelor's in business administration. School was always easy for me. I absorbed information like a sponge—and still do.

I capitalized on that from a young age, creating an app and software to protect anyone who is ever in need of protection. It led me to be where I am today—the CEO of Noble, a multibillion-dollar company.

Noble allows anyone to have the police and help at the press and release of a silent button. Whether you're walking to your car late at night or uncomfortable in a taxi ride, my app instructs you to press a button and hold it until the situation is no longer dangerous. Once you release it, you must enter a six-digit pin to disarm the counting-down alarm. If the time passes before the code is entered, police will be dispatched to your current location.

I have always had a passion for protecting those who need protection. That will never change.

Tonight's meeting will cover the numbers of users, the uptick of people who require law enforcement, and what the trend looks like moving forward and how we are going to be able to manage the continuing, growing use of Noble. We need to expand our team.

Once the app and software took off, we began to market to a new buyer. We developed an entire line of home and work systems that work similarly to the app. Versions of this tech existed previously, but not one that is this user friendly.

We sold out within minutes of the first launch, and we continue to do so each time. It took us a couple of years to build the manufacturing setup we have now, allowing us continual distribution of the product.

I am proud of my work and my company, but I loathe boring meetings that could easily take place without me.

I lock my house up and arm the alarm system before I walk to my McLaren Artura and get in. Breathing in the fresh and clean leather of my new car, I feel warmth bubble in my chest. I don't know if I feel love the same way others do, but the way I feel about this car has to be close.

I take off out of my driveway, grinning ear to ear as I race down the road, around the curve of the hill, and toward Melisse Restaurant—the place we're dining at tonight.

As much as I don't love the heat of California, the sunsets here are some of the most beautiful I've seen.

Within a few speedy minutes, I am parked and walking toward the entrance. It's a nice restaurant. I've dined here a few times. As I approach the front door, hearing each step I take click on the almost-empty side-walk, I check my other phone quickly to see if any of the monsters have answered my fake accounts. A mountain of messages is waiting.

"Shit," I mumble as I plow into someone's shoulders and my phone fumbles from my hand and onto the ground. Focusing my attention on the girl with her arms full of bags of groceries that have now spilled on the ground, I'm taken aback for a second, and I can't help but stare. She has dull black hair that lies flat on her head, cascading over her shoulders and down her back.

Her eyes, a blinding light-gray contrast from the darkness of her hair, flick up to mine, and a shy smile lifts her full lips.

My spine warms, and the sensation is almost

alarming.

"Are you okay?" I ask her as I gather her strewn groceries and rebag them hastily as she watches me with parted lips and downcast, flickering, widened eyes.

She nods but remains silent. My mouth dries, and tingles spread down my body.

"It was my fault. I was the one not paying attention. Will you make it home okay? I can arrange a ride if you need one," I offer genuinely.

She shouldn't be walking these streets alone at this time of night anyway. She has no idea of the monsters that lurk in the shadows.

She picks my phone up, glancing at the screen, and my pulse races. But when she hands it back to me, the screen is black, and my phone is locked.

Whew.

Again, she chooses to stay quiet and just shoos my offer away with her hand.

"Are you sure you're okay?" I ask her, surprising myself by how long I'm lingering.

She sets the bags on the ground and pulls out her phone, typing rapidly before showing me what she wrote.

I can't really talk. I'm sorry. I'm perfectly fine. Thank you. Have a good night.

Just like that, she takes a step past me, and her scent wafts toward me. The warmth at the base of my spine pulses, and I bite down on my cheek to stop myself from reaching out and grabbing her.

Why is my killer tingle going off because of her?

Her slightly disheveled look reminds me of the people I work so hard to protect. Could she be hiding a darkness behind those eyes? Could she be a monster that needs to be taken out?

"Mr. Noble," one of my associates pulls me from my stupor.

"Good evening, Elijah." I greet him with a feigned smile and follow him inside while my thoughts are still consumed by the girl on the street.

I need to find out why that reaction happened. I need to know why she is being marked by my moral compass as evil.

But unfortunately, I'm afraid her fate might be sealed either way. I won't be able to breathe properly again until I figure out what kind of monster she is, what darkness lies behind those eyes, and when I do, *she's mine.*

BIRD

TWO

When little girls make wishes upon stars, they wish for presents and princes to sweep them off of their feet, and perhaps I did the same before.

I've only ever wished to be free of my father.

I've thought about my death a lot throughout the years. I've even planned it countless times. I've held a knife to my wrist, a gun to my forehead, the brim of a pill bottle to my lips, but I could never actually follow through with it. No matter how much I begged myself to do it, my body refused.

At some point, I stopped trying. Although I think it might not matter if I pull the trigger. I'm already dead. I have been for years.

BIRD

I've always lived in silence, in the background and in the shadows of the world. I have kept to myself and found friendship with the thoughts in my head.

I'm forgettable, nothing worthy of remembering. At least that's what my father always tells me.

Life has never been something I've deemed worth living. I figure the world has a set amount of trauma and damage to dish out to the children, and I happen to have hit the lottery in both departments.

I was raised to accept the destiny my father laid out for me. I've never known anything else. It has only ever been him and me. My mother died when she gave birth to me—something my father never fails to remind me of any chance he gets. He molds me into whatever image he sees fit. He chooses how I dress, how I act, and sometimes, he even chooses when I breathe. Often, I feel like I'm just a puppet that he likes to take out of the closet and play with now and then. When the puppet doesn't act accordingly, it gets punished. I used to resist his punishments when I was younger, but I have learned it is easier for me if I go along with it and just take it.

Throughout the years, his choices of torment have altered—sometimes depending on his mood, sometimes depending on what's nearest to him when he snaps.

Much like a puppet, I feel mindless, void of life.

I don't know if *fog* is the right word to describe the mental haze that I constantly live in, but it feels like a good way to imagine it.

SILENCE AND SORROW

It's like I'm sitting in the dark, always watching a movie through my eyes that don't even feel like my own. Is it possible to be stuck inside of your body and be completely disconnected from it at the same time?

I need to learn how to break these fucking strings he has tethered to me.

But I might have found a start to figuring out how.

When I bumped into that businessman, some of the clouds faded away, forcing me closer to reality. I'm not sure what to think of it or what to do about it. It was like getting struck by lightning, like a wake-up call.

Thoughts and ideas began flowing through my mind like water breaking through a dam. I blinked, and suddenly, I wasn't eight years old, when my dad hit me for the first time. Like I'm finally aware that eleven years have come and gone, and I've been floating somewhere between barely conscious and dead.

Rushing past the post office, I turn onto my street and walk down the sidewalk, my pace quickening with each step. I think I'm going to be late.

Shit.

He told me to go straight to the grocery store and back. I have to prepare dinner, clean the house, and serve him. Now, I'm going to be late, which he hates.

My palms sweat as I race up my street to the house all the way on the far right, right next to the Dead End sign. *Poetic.*

BIRD

The bags feel like a million pounds by the time I reach the front door and throw it open.

"Elodie!" my father's voice booms through the house, rattling the photos on the wall. "Five minutes late."

He rushes into the entryway as I close the door behind me. My head whips to the side as the back of his hand strikes my cheek, and the all-too-familiar sting burns.

Keeping my eyes locked on the ground, I address him the way he prefers. "Sorry, sir. Someone ran into me on the way home, and it slowed me down. It won't happen again."

"It'd better not. Watch where you're going next time," he warns. "I have been saving lives all day. I come home and just want a warm meal, and you can't even do that."

He opens his arms and looks at the bags, and I pass them over to him. He sets them on the ground.

He kisses my forehead before sliding his fingers into my hair. He yanks my head back and drags me into the living room.

"I work day in and day out as one of the best general surgeons in this damn world, and my own daughter can't even show me a sliver of respect!" He shouts louder with each word.

"I'm sorry," I whisper, my apology seemingly genuine.

He releases me, and I rub my head to ease the pain from him trying to rip my scalp off.

"Good." He smiles without emotion. "Now, go make dinner. I'm starved."

Turning away from him, I race into the entryway to get the bags and get dinner made so I can go hide in my room the rest of the night in hopes that he forgets I exist.

My eyes burn, but for reasons other than the pulsing soreness on my cheek and head. I should have said something. I should have stood up to him. But I knew that would only end worse than behaving as he expects me to.

I walk into the kitchen and hastily unload the bags. Quickly, I get meatloaf made and shaped into the pan and begin boiling water for the potatoes before slipping away to the bathroom.

My father hasn't always been this way. He used to be kinder, warmer. He used to read me bedtime stories and tuck me in at night.

But at some point, something changed in him—or rather, maybe it was always there, and he finally chose to reveal it to me. Regardless, the first night he struck me down, I came face-to-face with the devil.

Each time he hit me or punished me, he took another piece of my soul. There's nothing left for him or anyone else to steal from me. He already took it all.

Zoning out until I'm dishing food onto our plates, I snap back to reality when my father's voice cuts through the room.

"Finally," he groans and sits at the head of the table.

Setting his plate down, I ask, "What would you like to drink?"

"Get me a glass of ice water," he responds, taking a small bite of his meatloaf.

I wonder how hard it would be to acquire poison to put in his food. Is something like that even accessible to the public? Do all poisons have a scent or a unique taste?

There's something severely wrong with all of this, isn't there? Have I managed to talk myself into thinking this is normal? Am I crazy?

"Delicious, sweetie. Thank you." My father pushes away from the table and walks back into the living room to sit in his spot on the sofa that I'm not allowed to sit on and work the rest of the evening.

"Thank you," I respond automatically.

Moving through the motions, I clean the kitchen and dining room until not a speck of dust or dirt can be found on the perfect hardwood floor before retiring to my room.

My father prefers to have the house to himself after dinner, and I couldn't be happier to follow that rule.

I quickly ascend the staircase and walk into my bedroom, gently shutting the door behind me.

This is my favorite time of the day, aside from my walks alone outside in the mornings. I lift the edge of my mattress up and pull out the ragged journal and pen.

This journal has seen better days, and I can't help but imagine all the journals lined up in a store, waiting for their owner to pick them up and take them home. Wondering what tales and stories of love and life will be poured into them. I'm afraid mine drew the short straw and would have preferred anyone else to have chosen it.

Opening the journal to the next blank page, I put my pen on the paper, take a deep breath, and let my being flow onto the page.

Two roses. Flowers of beauty and pain. A balance of good and bad. Do they enter this world with their ending already written, doomed to loneliness in the crack of a sidewalk, or are they granted a lush life in a bed alongside others?

A man walks along and plucks the red rose, deeming it too pretty to leave behind. He tells it how beautiful it is, how special before stripping it of its thorns and leaves, leaving it bare and vulnerable and exposed. Each day passes, and the man tells it less and less of its beauty as it withers, the petals shriveling and falling away, until death is all that remains. So, the man plucks another one.

A man walks along and spots a white rose. He remarks on its beauty, but instead of ripping it from its life source, he uproots it and plants it in a flourishing new home. He waters it and praises it from the moment he spots it until its very last.

Which rose am I? Which rose are you?

I might live in a nice house that most people dream about, but I would trade it for anything. I ran away once a few years ago, and unless I can be sure he can't find me, I won't do it again. He has the money and the resources. He told me he can find me anywhere, and I believe that to be true. He did it once before after all, and I won't endure those punishments again.

Either way, I'm going to find a way out of this hell.

SILENCE AND SORROW

BIRD

KALIUS

THREE

Sex is a pleasure that I tentatively indulge in. It's messy. Not the act itself, but everything that comes afterward. They always want more. More attention. More touch and affection. I want the opposite, so I often opt out of the interaction altogether and manage my needs on my own.

Attraction is just another feeling. I'm not a complete sociopath. I have feelings and urges like everyone else. But unlike everyone else, I control them. I can flip it off like a switch inside of me, dismissing any emotion. There is one urge that I can't resist, one that takes over my body, my senses, my being until it is let out to play, and that is the urge to kill.

BIRD

I used to fight it, telling myself that it was wrong and immoral. That I shouldn't have the need to do these things, that I could control this desire too. But I think I was just born this way.

When I was little, I used to kill insects, any kind I could get my hands on. I liked taking them apart, inspecting every tiny little detail of their bodies before discarding them.

Everyone always says that killing animals at a young age is one of the signs of the Macdonald triad. But I never killed anything other than bugs—at least until I turned eighteen. Homicide is the only box I ever checked of the Macdonald triad, if bugs count as animals that is.

The first person I ever killed was my father. A pathetic excuse for a human being. He'd deserved what was coming to him—hell, he'd been asking for it for years. He treated people like shit, like garbage on the bottom of his shoe. Including the rotating door of women who entered and left our home—the kind you pay for and discard, not the kind you keep.

Life is a game of power. That is what my father taught me from an early age. Power can come in many forms. Money. Sex. Strength.

You can earn it, or you can take it. But the outcome for either path is the same. I chose to take what I want in life, at any cost to anyone else, and I've never regretted it.

SILENCE AND SORROW

In fact, I don't think there is a single choice that I've made that I regret. Why would I? Regret is for weak-minded people who would rather mull over past decisions instead of moving forward and focusing on the present and future.

That stark black hair flashes in my vision, and I lick my bottom lip before sucking it between my teeth and biting down. Never have I been unable to dismiss attraction for a woman, although I'm not sure that's what it is.

Her hair was a mess, clothes deeply worn and tattered. She reeked of desperation and despair. Not exactly what usually draws me in.

She is far too easy of a target. There would be no fight, no challenge.

Where is the fun in that?

I don't take pleasure in hurting the vulnerable—I will leave that to the other monsters in this world. Which is why my interest in this girl is so surprising to me. It doesn't make sense. She resembles the people I protect, and I've never had an issue managing any kind of feelings toward them.

She is already affecting me more than I'd like, pulling all my thoughts away from this meeting.

Shifting in my chair, I wish more than anything that this dinner would end. These pointless discussions don't need to involve me.

BIRD

Tuning back in to the conversation, I hear Bethany make a comment about our incredible company.

I suppose I am expected to act the part of the all-important and mighty CEO—a character I break out almost daily.

There are many characters I play—or rather, masks that I wear. They alter slightly depending on who I'm conversing with. I play into their personality and cater my behavior to them.
Every single word I say and expression I make is calculated. It is all a performance. Manipulation is a skill I have always mastered, even more so in adulthood.

Regardless of the numerous feelings and personas I replicate, there is one thing I rarely pretend to be. A nice guy.

Do I run a company that benefits the vulnerable people of our society? *Yes.*

Do I donate thousands and thousands of dollars every year to charities and organizations that are in the same fight as us? *Yes.*

Does Bethany's perfume irritate me enough to send me into a murderous rage? If I don't leave soon enough, it just might.

I can't stand that flowery, musky perfume. It reminds me of old ladies, and I fucking hate it. I can physically feel my dick withering in my pants.

Sighing, I show my annoyance for the irrelevant meeting.

SILENCE AND SORROW

"Send me the minutes after the meeting." I push my chair back into the table and throw on my jacket.

"If you don't mind, I'll be leaving for the night," I interrupt Bethany and kick my chair back, rising to my feet.

As if their minuscule opinions would change my decision, I allow a moment of silence for any interjections.

"Are you feeling ill, sir?" Bethany asks, and I clench my jaw at the condescending playfulness in her tone.

"Physically ill? No. Sick of this meeting? Yes." I chuckle lightheartedly, and the table joins in as if I was actually joking. "I have a meeting in the morning with Westhurt about a potential buyout for their company. I will be retiring from this dinner a bit early. Unless anyone has any objections?"

Slowly, I meet every single person's gaze with a blank stare. As I expect, they offer sweet goodbyes and good luck at the meeting tomorrow.

"Good night, everyone. Bethany?" I address her.

She bats her lashes at me and asks, "Yes, sir?"

Turning away, I leave without waiting for her response. I know she will feel the absence of it, the rejection. She is so sensitive and frail. It's amazing she's lasted this long as my executive assistant. She knows her place better than to attempt to mock me in front of these men.

BIRD

She's just lucky I don't take my anger out on women. Before I am even a foot out of the restaurant, I cancel my meetings for the next week.

I think I might be under the weather after all. A sickness is coming on, and I am going to find out everything there is to know about what's causing it—*her*.

It took me less than a day to find the mystery girl. After all, I did have the name of the grocery store she shopped at. It was only a matter of time before she returned. There was, of course, the chance that she stopped at this store as a onetime thing, but the odds of that were so low. Humans are creatures of habit—they can't help it. They frequent the same stores, the same coffee shops, the same anything. I find that it is exceptionally more so in women.

I was hoping that my new obsession would be showing up in a car; it would have been much easier to find out who she was if she had. A quick license plate run, and I would have had all the information I needed.

But of course, my little mystery wouldn't make it that easy for me.

When I finally spot her approaching on foot, I'm struck a little by her features. She's quite beautiful. I watch her enter the store and exit not ten minutes later.

I follow her home discreetly, careful to stay a safe distance away in my car.

I must say she is rather unaware of her surroundings. I pass her twice, and that should be enough to raise an alarm bell in her mind. But nothing about her body language changes.

Her posture doesn't straighten, she doesn't look around more than before, she doesn't call anyone. She doesn't do anything that someone who is being stalked home should do.

For someone who lives in this part of town, I'm surprised she doesn't have a car, let alone three or four different ones. I own a lot of real estate. It's easy profit to buy out homes and apartment buildings and rent them out. Aside from the initial buy, it takes almost none of my time. I give a rental agency ten percent of the profit, and they handle everything as the acting landlord. I know for a fact that the houses in this neighborhood run about one-point-five million. Which raises even more questions in my mind about this girl.

I park on the side of the street she turns off of and wait to see which house she walks into. The last one on the right side. I take a note of the house number and snap a picture on my phone before putting my phone down and taking one last look at her.

Again, I am puzzled and lost for reasons for my newfound fascination. I can always manage whatever I am feeling at any time, aside from the occasional urge to kill. Even then, I make the decision on when it will happen.

It's like a thump in my chest that beats louder and harder, telling me it needs a release. I know that it won't go away until I feed the beast inside of me.

SILENCE AND SORROW

BIRD

FOUR

It has been four days since I first ran into my little mystery. I now know her name is Elodie Bardot. She is nineteen years old. She is an only child. Mother deceased. Her father is alive and living in the home with her. He is a well-known surgeon who was last year's recipient of the Distinguished Service Award. He has no record, and he's seemingly a well-liked and respected guy.

It looks like Elodie attended public school until seventh grade, but then there is no further record of public school. From what I can tell, she is not enrolled in any university either. Is she educated more than seventh grade? Did her father teach her? Did he hire someone? I'll find out in time.

BIRD

Elodie leaves her house twice a day at the exact same times. Once in the late morning at eleven fifteen for a walk. She travels two miles before turning around and returning home. Her path has not wavered a single step any of the three times I have followed her. The second time she leaves her house is at four thirty p.m. She walks to the grocery store, the same one from before, is inside for about ten minutes, then walks back home. Her father arrives home not ten minutes after her each day.

I was hoping that I could find out a lot about her online, but she has no social media whatsoever. Aside from helping a lady pick up the groceries she spilled on the ground, nothing about her routine changes. She leaves the house only two times daily. She is impeccably … *boring*.

From where my SUV is parked on the end of the street, I have a straight sight line into her bedroom, and she notoriously leaves the curtains open. Seriously, she should be more careful about her privacy. Who knows what creep could be looking in her windows?

Her father is leaving for the day, and then she'll be all alone. When the doctor pulls out of the driveway, I redirect my attention to Elodie. She is staring out of the window, watching him leave. I wonder if she cares for him. I know what it's like to have a father and not love him.

By the sharp daggers in her eyes as she stares at him backing out of the driveway, I think I might already have my answer.

Her hair is pulled into a tight ponytail, dangling past her neck and onto the back of her oversize black T-shirt.

She sits down on her bed, and I can't look away from the beauty of her, the sharpness of her cheek-bones and jawline. She has an elegance to her that I've been ignoring. She's graceful, and every step she takes is intentional. I can't help but be mesmerized by her.

She stands up and kicks her little shorts off, which I didn't notice were hidden beneath her shirt. Hooking her fingers under the hem of the black shirt, she lifts it up and off of her body, leaving only a purple bra and panties. Which quickly join her top and bottoms on the ground.

My dick throbs at the sight of her bare tits. Has she ever had a man deep inside that little pussy of hers? What about her ass?

The thought of anyone else claiming her body makes my throat burn, surprising me.

Is that ... jealousy?

It doesn't matter how many have come before; no one touches her but me now, in any capacity. Until I decide what her fate will be, she is off-limits to the world.

How good would her lips feel, stretched around

my thick cock?

Unzipping my jeans, I free my hard shaft from my pants and wrap my fingers tightly around it.

Fuck.

She bends over to pick her clothes up, giving me a perfect view of her bare cunt and ass. I bet it would look so good, reddened from my hand or belt.

I pump myself harder and harder as I stare at my sweet little Elodie. So naive, so innocent-looking. A blank canvas for me to paint with my desires and wickedness. An image of her face dripping with my come flashes in my mind, nearly hurtling me over the edge.

Without pulling my gaze away from her, I picture her bent over my table in my basement, with her hands tied in front of her, keeping her in place. Oh the things I could show her, do to her.

My basement is a death sentence, so the mere thought of having her in my most vulnerable space has me about to explode. No one walks out of that basement alive besides myself. She wouldn't be different— she can't be.

As I continue to run my hand up and down my engorged cock, I cup my balls with my other hand and tug gently.

Fuck, I'm close.

"Elodie." Her name is a haunting whisper on my lips, which becomes my undoing.

Coming into my hand, I groan as I release all of

my pent-up desire. I wipe it off of my hand with a napkin from my console.

Feeling anew, I look at her with fresh eyes. My need to know her, my need to obsess over her, has to end. I can't live in this vehicle, watching her forever.

She is inhibiting my ability to be just, to be righteous, to rid this world of scum. As long as she's around, I am weak.

Maybe I just need to kill this infatuation before it gets worse, and there is only one way to do it.

Leaving her alone won't be enough. I won't be able to resist coming back. It won't matter if she runs or hides; I will find her. There isn't a cave or corner in this world where she can evade me.

I'll make it as quick and painless as possible. She will be a sacrifice for the greater good. It's for the best. It's not fair to subject her to my never-ending hunting, it wouldn't be fair to either of us.

Starting my SUV, I pull away from the curb and head home. My skin electrifies at the thought of what is to come, and I push any second thoughts of taking her innocent life away. This is a onetime thing and a necessary evil.

I need to go get everything ready in my basement, and I need to grab a few things to help me bring my Elodie home.

BIRD

The second she is out of sight and on her walk, I step out of my van and stride to her front door. Lifting the welcome mat, I grab the key that she keeps stowed there. I saw her use it to get back in after her walks. I unlock the door and put the key back where I grabbed it from.

I want to do a quick tour of her house, gather any more information about her that I can before she returns. The aesthetic of the decor is simple. White, black, and gray color the rooms, similar to my own home.

I continue down the echoing hallway and find the staircase that leads to the second floor, where Elodie's room is.

Silently, I ascend the hardwood stairs and find her bedroom. Pushing the door open, I inhale deeply until I am overwhelmed by her scent. Sweet hints of vanilla and peaches. I bet she tastes as good as she smells.

I rummage through her drawers and pack a few of the pieces of clothing that I like, including a couple of pretty lace bra and panty sets.

SILENCE AND SORROW

Fuck. An image of her stretched out in front of me with her back arched in this little black set has my dick throbbing against my zipper.

Killing her right away would be a waste of both of our time. I want to talk to her and hopefully figure out what about her caught the attention of the Grim Reaper.

Moving over to her bed, I lift it up—because if she has anything to hide, there's a good chance it's under here, as I have yet to find anything hidden in her drawers or closet.

Bingo.

Pulling out the notebook that's wedged between the mattress and the wall, I smile. This is exactly what I wanted to find.

Flipping through the pages, I find something that I definitely wasn't expecting.

Utter darkness fills this journal. Poetry and raw, dark thoughts decorate every line.

Sitting down on her bed, I read a few entries. Laying my head down against her pillow, I'm completely surrounded by her scent, and it pulls a primal, animalistic urge out of me.

After reading a few poems, I hear the door downstairs unlock, and my adrenaline spikes, as I know what's about to happen.

Throwing my legs over the side of the bed, I sit up and set her journal next to me, tapping my fingers on the cover. My pulse races with excitement as I hear her steps growing louder with each second.

Her head is down, looking at the apple in her hand, and she doesn't notice me right away as she crosses the threshold of the door.

When she looks up, her eyes widen, and she gasps as she drops the apple. I reach out and catch it. I expect her to scream, but unfortunately, she doesn't. "Hello, my sweet," I murmur and hand the apple out to her.

She doesn't take it. Instead, she turns and tries to run out of the door.

Poor thing. She thinks she has a chance to get away.

I snatch her wrist and spin her back around, kicking the door shut behind her in one swift movement.

"Ooh, *so* close," I mock her and position myself between her and the door. "I'm afraid this isn't a fair fight."

Slipping my fingers into my pocket, I grab the needle and pop the cap off, tucking the cap back into my pocket.

"Easy way or hard way? Know that this is going into your skin regardless. But it can either be basically painless or more painful. Your choice," I say, flicking the top of the needle.

She remains silent, and her hands start trembling.

Her lips part, and she tries to say something, but only an inaudible whisper comes out.

Clicking my tongue, I make the decision for her. "Stand still, and it will be over in just a second."

SILENCE AND SORROW

I stride forward, but she tries to go around me, and I grab her by the arm and pull her into me. Leaning her back against my chest, I secure her with my free hand and crush her against me. She thrashes and fights me with more strength than I anticipate, but it's not enough to make a difference in the outcome.

I pull us to the ground and sit down, positioning her between my legs and caging her in.

"Little poke here," I warn her before I slide the needle into her arm and inject the ketamine, tucking the needle by my side afterward. "You are going to hallucinate. What you see won't be real." My lips press into the top of her head, my sudden show of affection surprising me. "You'll be back to normal in a few hours."

She continues to thrash in my grasp. She bounces against my lap, and my dick twitches. Moments later, her fighting seems to slow, and she falls still.

KALIUS

FIVE

I have never been happier with my decor choices in this basement before now. There are many aspects of my kill room, but my favorite is the viewing room, which is hidden behind the one-way mirror, where I'm watching her from now. I rearranged the space a bit. I unbolted my metal table and moved it to the edge of the room. In its place is a long chain that connects to the leather locked collar around her neck.

She is lying on a mattress on the floor, still stuck in the drug-induced K-hole—a state between intoxication and a coma caused by the amount of ketamine I gave her. It's been about an hour since I injected her, so she should be returning to reality shortly.

BIRD

I spent a few more minutes gathering stuff from her house once I had her loaded into the SUV, which I'd backed into her garage. I grabbed a few files from the doc's home office that had been locked in a drawer in his desk. It'd only taken me a second to pick it. I also took some of the products in her bathroom, including a peach-vanilla lotion that I'd found next to the matching perfume.

For some reason, those scents—*her scent*—make me feral. In case I keep her around for a little while, I want to have it available.

Elodie begins to stir on the silk-sheet-covered mattress. Her fingers twitch and lift to her face. She rubs her eyes and yawns. Watching every part of her animate back to life is fascinating. She hasn't registered that she is chained to the floor of my basement.

Her eyes flutter open, and for a brief second, she takes in her surroundings. Then, panic takes over. She sucks in a sharp breath and throws herself up, her hand flying to her stomach. High ketamine doses can cause some stomach pains, but they'll subside in a couple of hours, if not sooner.

Pressing the button that turns my microphone on, I talk into it. "Take a deep breath. The stomach cramps will go away soon."

She jumps at the sound of my voice and looks around for the source. The fear in her eyes makes my dick pulse, and I can't help but scan down her body, admiring her black lace set that I changed her into.

SILENCE AND SORROW

I'd considered leaving her there naked, but I thought I could offer her a shred of decency. Her breathing quickens, and she tucks her knees to her chest.

Her eyes scour the room, and her bottom lip trembles. I'm sure this scene is very overwhelming. I could talk her through it, ease her anxiety. But watching her squirm is far too enjoyable.

While sitting here and staring at her through this glass is great, I know what will be even better. Pushing the office chair, I wheel it to the door, twist the knob, kick the door open, and step into the game we are about to play.

"Hello, Elodie," I sing to her in a deep tone.

Her head whips in my direction, and she jumps backward, away from me. I roll the chair into the room, stopping a few feet away from her, and take a seat.

There is so much I want to know about her. I'm not quite sure where to start. If I want her to communicate openly and honestly, I need to ensure she is at least comfortable.

"Do you need anything? Water?" I offer her.

She stares at me with wide eyes and whispers something, but I can't make it out.

"Speak up." I tell her.

Her face drops, and she glares at me.

She whispers again, "I can't, asshole."

Sassy.

"Are you sick?" I ask her, leaning forward and putting my elbows on my knees.

She shakes her head.

"Did you have an accident?"

Before she can respond, I walk over to my desk in the corner and grab a notebook and pen.

Retracing my steps, I hand her the writing tools and sit back down in my chair.

She studies me for a moment before turning to a blank page and writing. Whipping the notebook around, she holds it up for me to see.

I can only whisper.

"Why?" I prod for more information.

She glares at me again.

I chuckle at her stubbornness. Most people in this situation would be pleading and crying, not glaring at me in annoyance.

"Let me make something clear to you. You are alive right now because I want to get to know you before I decide what to do with you. So, if you would rather keep all the blood in your body, I suggest you cooperate with me."

She considers what I said before she starts writing again.

My dad said I was in an accident as a baby, and

my vocal cords got severed. I couldn't tell you exactly how. I don't remember. Because I was a BABY.

The fact that her written words hold as much sarcasm as her whispers pulls the corners of my lips up.

"Tell me about your childhood," I instruct her.

She shrugs, and I sigh. There has to be a faster way to get the information I need.

She flips the notebook around.

What do you want to know?

Leaning forward, I cup her chin and she doesn't pull away. "*Everything.*"

Something is seriously wrong with me. What is she doing to me? What am I doing with her?

This poison that she has placed in my mind is driving me insane. I can't stop thinking about her or obsessing over her. I want to know what her lips taste like, what her body feels like grinding against mine. I want to know how her body reacts from coming over and over again.

Again with this damn infatuation. The urges I have for her feel too familiar to the ones I have for my victims. But I never wondered how Robert's mouth would feel when stretched around my cock. I wanted to know what his tongue looked like when cut out of his throat.

BIRD

Whatever I am feeling for her is different. Part of me wants to end this, rid the world of the one person who has ever infected me with these feelings. But I can't bring myself to do it yet, not before I sink my cock into her little pussy.

With her face still cupped in my hand, I lift her chin. "Get on your knees."

She obeys me, kneeling before me. Pleasure runs down my spine and straight into my dick. I want her to choke on it with my fist in her hair.

I slam my eyes shut to remind myself that I'm not one of the monsters that I hunt. I don't take advantage of the vulnerable.

I stroke her cheek and run my hand through her hair. "I want to know everything there is to know about you, Elodie. Introduce me to your demons. Tell me your favorite things in the world. Tell me what scares you, what drives you. What pleases you. I want to know you inside and out."

Next to the fear in her eyes is a glimmer that pulses at my words.

She whispers, "And then you'll kill me?"

"And then I'll decide what to do with you." I release her from my grasp. "I have to run a couple of errands. Are you hungry?"

She remains still, then slowly nods.

"Any allergies?" I ask her as I stand and walk backward, pushing my chair back to my viewing room.

She shakes her head.

SILENCE AND SORROW

"Any requests?" I keep my full attention on her, waiting for her response.

She shakes her head again.

"All right, I'll be back soon. If you need to use the bathroom, your chain will let you reach it. Don't waste your energy trying to escape or find a weapon—you won't."

I shove the chair in my viewing room and walk up the stairs, locking the basement behind me.

A piece of garbage named Jerry was next on my list, but I didn't intend on continuing my extracurriculars until I dealt with Elodie. But he's given me no choice.

The thump the predator's body makes when falling down the stairs is equivalent to a grenade going off in the room. Each bang louder than the last. Elodie must have fallen back asleep since I left, but she sure isn't sleeping anymore.

I follow him down the stairs and walk over to Elodie and hand the food bags to her.

She looks up at me graciously and accepts the bag

of burgers and fries, digging in immediately.

Returning my attention back to the guy that has now stopped rolling, I walk over and grab the back of his shirt and drag him over to my table.

Rapid tapping behind me grabs my attention. I turn to see Elodie practically slapping her notebook.

What are you doing? Who is he?

"You'll find out shortly, I promise."

I grunt as I continue to move his almost two-hundred-pound body into position.

Grabbing the remote for my table, I press the release button, and the table begins whirring. One side of the table starts lifting in the air. This allows me to easily load and unload it. Once the hydraulics finish tilting it, I grab the cuffs and chains dangling from the top and lock them around his wrists and neck. Once they are secured in place, I clasp the other two around his ankles.

I press the other button, and the hydraulics start back up, cranking the chains and dragging his body up onto the table before lowering itself back down until it's flat again.

Tapping pulls my attention back to the black-haired beauty behind me. She waves her notebook around.

Hello!!! What is going on?!

"Do you know who I am, Elodie?" I take a few steps closer to her.

She shakes her head.

I close the distance between us and brush her hair away from her face. She doesn't shy away or flinch, surprising me yet again.

A realization that I think I have just been ignoring hits me. She can't leave this room. She's seen my face. She's about to know my name. She is a liability to my survival. Just because she can't leave doesn't mean she has to die.

You can't.

If I kept her for my own pleasure, I would be just as bad as Jerry Gandry, who is lying on my table across the room.

Pushing those thoughts once again out of my mind, I focus on the present and not the potential future.

"My name is Kalius Noble. Have you heard of Noble Security?" I ask her.

She nods and begins to write.

Yeah. It's the brand of our cameras at home.

"Yeah, it sure is. It was easy enough to hack your account and shut all the cameras off during my visit." I take a step back and glance at Jerry.

She writes again and shows me.

That doesn't explain your dungeon.

I laugh—a real laugh—at the word *dungeon.*
"You will learn the rest about me in time. But what you should always keep in mind is although I might do bad things, I am not a bad guy. In fact, I am the opposite."

Kidnapping me was you being a good guy?

"No, Elodie. You are the one exception to my righteousness thus far. I took you because I wanted to. I'm not yet sure if it was the right or wrong thing to do. First, I have to discover which side you belong on—the monster hunters or the monsters."
Jerry groans, and we both look his way.
"His name is Jerry, and without a doubt, he falls under the category of monster."
Jerry cries out, "What's going on? Where am I?"
"Elodie," I say to her, grabbing her attention.
She looks at me with confusion.
"Should Jerry live or die?" I ask her straightforwardly.
She stares at me with upturned eyes and parted lips. She slowly starts shaking her head, and her lips form the word *no.*
"Elodie," I scold her, "the options are live or die. Which will you choose?"
She aggressively turns the page, ripping it in two.

She discards it and writes on the next page.

Live.

"Jerry, tell her why you're here." My voice shifts, deep and chilling.

He whimpers like the little baby he is. "I-I don't know, m-man. I d-don't know!"

I repeat what I know about him by memory to Elodie. "Jerry Gandry. Forty-eight years old. Married to wife, Stacy. No kids. *Thank God.* He's a car salesman." I turn and focus my attention to Jerry. "Now, Jerry, tell Elodie here how we met."

"He's crazy! He broke into my home and hit me over the head, and I woke up here!" he shouts.

"Tsk-tsk," I growl. "Jerry, how do you know Emilia Miller?"

His face drops, and he turns ghostly white. "I-I don't know who you're talking about."

"Sure you don't," I snark.

Ripping my phone out of my pocket, I find the messages he sent to a supposed eleven-year-old girl.

Giving Elodie my trust, I hand my phone out to her.

Her wide eyes flick up to me, and her lips part. She knows I'm giving it to her and counting on her not to do anything stupid, like call the police.

"See for yourself," I softly say to her. "He believes

the person he was talking to was an eleven-year-old girl."

As she reads through the vulgar and abrasive messages he sent me, she covers her mouth in disgust and whispers, "Oh my God."

"Scroll down and read the last message he sent," I tell her. Then, I address the monster across the room, my voice growing louder and angrier with each word. "Jerry, tell us about your marriage—or rather about the bruises that always decorate your wife's body. Tell us how you have an obsession with and an attraction to *children*. Tell us about your previous victims—all thirteen of them."

Jerry is a stuttering buffoon. "I-I d-don't know wh-what you're ta-talking about!"

Elodie stares up at me with watery eyes—the first time I've seen her cry. She is so fucking beautiful when she cries.

Her arm stretches up, and she hands me the phone.

I read the last text he sent aloud. "*Do you want to have a playdate today? I have another girl your age at my house who would love to meet you! Her name is Maggie.*"

Gazing down at Elodie, I say, "What Jerry left out about how we met is that I found Maggie tied up in his closet and drugged. Don't worry; Maggie is now safe and sound with her family."

SILENCE AND SORROW

The look in Elodie's light-gray eyes isn't one of fear; it is admiration. As much as I want to greedily soak that in, I don't feel deserving of it. I am not something to be admired. If she knew the things I had done, she wouldn't look at me so kindly.

"I c-can explain!" Jerry shrieks, and I shoot daggers his way to silence him.

My murderous glare stays locked on Jerry. "Elodie, I will ask you again. Should Jerry live or die?"

She taps my side, and I give her my full attention. She flips the notebook around for me to read.

Why are you making me choose?

"Because, my sweet, I value your opinion. It means more to me than you could know." I brush the backs of my fingers across her cheek.

She writes in the notebook again and shows me her final answer.

Die.

"That's my girl," I hum.

"What did she say?" Jerry shouts. "Please don't hurt me!"

"Jerry, Jerry, Jerry …" I trail off and take a few slow steps his way, feeling a warmth wash over me. "How many little girls did you hurt?"

"Please! Please don't do this!" he whimpers.

"How many, Jerry? This is the last time I will ask nicely," I warn.

"Th-thirteen," he mumbles.

"Try again," I snap as I walk over to my tool wall and decide what to use first.

Picking up my favorite knife, I gaze into the reflection of the blade.

I answer for him, as he can't seem to find the words. "Thirteen, plus Maggie, so fourteen, Jerry. Did you *already* forget about Maggie?"

"I never touched her!"

Spinning around, I rush to the head of the table and press the blade into his neck, spitting my words into his face. "Do you think what you did won't cause her any trauma?" I mock him. "*I never touched her!* You are a pathetic waste of humanity."

Pressing down on the blade, I draw blood. The droplets roll down his neck and pool on the table beneath him.

He shrieks and once again pleads for his life, like his words can alter what is already set in stone. "I'm sorry! Please!"

Leaning down, I whisper into his ear, "Too late."

Walking around to the side of the table, I look him in the eyes and announce his fate, "I will punish you for every little girl you hurt. For your fourteen victims, you will feel my blade penetrate you fourteen times."

He begins to cry, as all of them usually do. "Please. I'm b-begging you."

"Please keep pleading for your life. I love hearing people cry on this table."

Bringing the knife up in the air, I inhale and funnel the anger inside of me into the swing of the knife.

I plunge it down and feel it slice into the flesh of his groin.

He screams out in pain, and I can't stop the smile that pulls my lips up.

Ripping the knife out of him causes his body to buck, blood to spray, and I laugh.

"How does it feel to be violated?"

My own words spark fury inside of me. This piece of garbage has done such heinous things in his life.

With speed, I bring the knife up and plunge it down into his outer ribs. A frenzy takes over me, and I slice into him again and again, focusing on places that will cause less blood loss. I want him to be conscious for this.

Blood spews around us as I deliver blow after blow. My breathing quickens, and I am working up a sweat by the time he receives his tenth gash.

His screams haven't quieted one bit; if anything, they've intensified with each blow. Forcing in a deep breath, I exhale and slam the knife to the table.

"Goddammit, Jerry! You got blood on my shirt!"

I shout with a smile on my face. With a deep chuckle, I say, "I'm not upset, Jerry. I would consider myself a failure if these walls weren't decorated with your blood when I was finished."

Bunching the back of my shirt up, I lift it over my head and toss it on the ground.

Unable to resist, I glance back at Elodie. I expect her to be cowering behind her pillow or notebook, but instead, I find her watching me, her eyes scanning down my bare back.

"Like what you see?" I tease her.

She looks away as her cheeks darken.

Who the hell is this girl? Why isn't she afraid?

Returning my attention back to Jerry, I pick my knife back up.

He's growing weaker, which is understandable from his loss of blood. I don't know how much longer he'll stay awake, so let's end this.

"I w-won't tell anyone," Jerry says, his voice weak and fragile.

"Oh, Jerry, it wouldn't matter if I let you go; you wouldn't survive anyway." I playfully sigh and jab the blade into his side, feeling it scrape against a bone inside him. Blood sprays all over me as I rip the knife out of him.

Flipping the knife in my hand, I wrap my fingers around the hilt and sink the blade into his thigh.

"How many is that, Jerry?" I ask him as I wipe the

blood off of the blade with my fingers.

"I-I don't know …" His voice trails off.

I land another blow to him, driving the knife into the flesh above his collarbone.

Huffing as I stab him, I say, "Thirteen. Which means there's only one left. Sad. I could have done this with you forever, Jerry."

Walking to the head of the table, I place my hands on either side of his head. "Any requests for the last one?"

"I-I'm sor—"

"I don't give a shit." I drag the knife across his throat, cutting him off.

Blood pools from his throat as he coughs and hacks. Within seconds, the coughing ceases, and he goes still.

Breathing heavily from the adrenaline coursing through me, I turn to face Elodie.

She is sitting on her knees and watching me with a curious stare.

"Are you scared of me?" I walk over to her.

She scans down my bloody chest, making my dick twitch with excitement.

She begins writing in her notebook and shows me.

I should be.

She stands up and I close the distance between us.

BIRD

She looks up at me, and her lips part as she whispers, "But I'm not."

SILENCE AND SORROW

BIRD

SIX

I might be the dumbest person in the world for it, but regardless, it's the truth. I'm not afraid of him.

I've lived with an abusive man my whole life. He would hit me for speaking against his opinions or values. He punished me for stepping out of line and not conforming to his rules. He beat me down until I had no thoughts of my own. I walked the way he wanted me to walk; I talked when he allowed me to. He controlled every aspect of my life.

Somehow, being chained in this basement is the freest I have ever felt. My dad has looked at me as *less than* my entire life, always looking through me. Kalius looks at me, and he *sees* me.

Did he just murder that man in front of me? *Yes.*

Was that man deserving of his punishment for whatever ungodly things he had done to those children? *Every second of it.*

Does what Kalius did make him a bad person? I don't know. But if it does, then I suppose I'm right there with him since I chose for that man to die.

Now, Kalius is standing in front of me, blood dripping down his chest, and a warmth I'm not used to pulses through my core. His chest and abdomen are ripped, and I can't keep my eyes off of him.

He was created to attract people to him. Like a bright light you can't help but go to. His beauty is a weapon, and he wields it with confidence. His dark hair, parted in the middle, falls to both sides of his forehead, and my fingers tingle to run through it and brush it out of his face.

His dark eyes bore into me, and it dawns on me that I'm sitting here in my bra and panties—a different set that I was in when I returned home from my walk. He must have changed me. I can't believe he saw me naked, as no man has before.

Did he like what he saw?

Is he pumping some kind of drug into this room to turn me on? Because how, in my right mind, am I focusing on what his hands felt like on my body when I passed out and not the dead body across the room?

I can't help it. He is electrifying me. I can't tear my

stare away from his eyes, his full lips, the sharpness of his jaw, or the cute curve of his nose.

What would it be like to be his?

My tongue swipes my bottom lip of its own accord, and his eyes drop to my parted lips.

"What am I going to do with you, Elodie?" he groans.

"Hopefully not put me on that table," I whisper softly.

He smirks. "There are other things I could do to you while you were strapped to that table."

Vulnerability sweeps across my cheeks, and I look down and away from his intense stare.

"Would you like that? To be fucked on there, knowing what has happened on it?" he hums, almost moaning at his words.

Slowly lifting my stare, I swallow hard when I see the bulge growing in his now-tight jeans.

I shrug. "I don't know."

He takes another step toward me. "You don't know, huh? Do I make you nervous?"

I shiver as a tingle slithers down my spine. I nod.

His fingers reach out and lift my chin up while his other hand stretches around my neck, right underneath my jawline.

My breathing hitches and quickens.

"Are you a dirty girl, Elodie? In the days I watched you, I never saw you touch yourself or meet anyone for a hookup. Surely, you've masturbated before?" he asks me, his voice deep and gruff.

Nodding, I answer truthfully, "Yes."

His grip tightens, and he brings his lips inches from mine. "Have you ever been fucked? Has anyone ever made you feel like you're levitating, like fireworks are bursting inside your entire body, like your orgasm is taking over every cell in your body and erupting with pleasure?"

I'm practically panting as I shake my head.

His eyes darken. "You've never let anyone touch you?"

Again, I shake my head.

"Would you let me?" he growls against my mouth.

I'm on fire, and there isn't anything I want more than what he is offering. "Yes. If you want to."

"If I *want* to?" he scoffs and grips my throat tighter, and a shock of pleasure shoots through my body. "I can't stop thinking about it. I am a man of control and precision, yet you have thrown a wrench in my entire goddamn life. You don't consume my thoughts; you *are* my *every thought*. I don't want to touch you. I need to devour you and feel you. I will greedily take every part of your body until all you know is me, all you want is *me*."

I've always imagined losing my virginity to a boyfriend I love, not a killer on a mattress in his basement. But I'm so fucking turned on right now. I need to feel him.

All I can manage to do is nod. I'm unable to form a single fucking word.

He sucks my bottom lip between his teeth and tugs. I exhale sharply.

"Do you realize how dangerous it is to be the center of my obsession?"

He releases me and storms off, exiting into the room behind the mirror without another word.

"Fuck," I whisper and roll my eyes.

I sit down on the mattress as incoherent noise sounds through the speakers.

Oh my God.

It's his breathing.

"Fuuuck," he moans into the microphone, breathing heavily.

Turning to face the mirror, I try to look through it even though I know it's impossible. I lock eyes with my reflection and am taken aback.

Is it possible to change drastically over the course of a few hours? The girl staring back at me has an aura of confidence about her, a sparkle in her eyes that I've never seen in the mirrors of my own home.

The door kicks open. He steps through, and I sharply inhale.

His pants are gone. The only clothing that remains are the boxers that are fighting for their life not to tear apart from his ginormous bulge.

"I still haven't decided if you are going to live or die, Elodie." His deep voice cuts through the heavy silence.

I gulp, knowing that whatever he chooses is out of my hands and out of my control.

He cups himself and takes a step toward me. "Keeping you alive is as dangerous for me as it is for you."

Gripping my pen and paper, I write.

Can I just stay down here?

His eyebrows pinch, and he takes another step. "You want to stay chained in this basement, like my little pet?"

Rather than return home to my father? Yes. Ten times over. I think my chances of dying are the same no matter where I am, either by the hands of Kalius or my father.

Yes. I'll be good.

He chuckles deep in his throat, and it sends chills down my body.

He closes the distance between us and grabs my jaw. "You wanna be my good little pet?"

Slowly, I nod and lick my lips.

"Why on earth would you agree to that?" he questions genuinely.

SILENCE AND SORROW

I whisper, "I can't go home. I would rather you kill me than let me go home."

His thumb swipes across my wet bottom lip. "Why?"

Swallowing hard, I answer him truthfully, "My father. You asked me if I'm a monster or a monster hunter. It's more complicated than that. I'm neither. I'm the prey."

His voice goes cold. "He touches you? Hurts you?"

My skin crawls at the question. "Never sexually. But, yes, he hits me. Punishes me."

Flashes of his *punishments* play in my eyes. The years of torment and pain that man has caused me. Everyone loves him, looks up to him, admires him. It disgusts me.

I couldn't do it anymore. I needed to find a way out. I needed a hunter.

Which is why I planned this.

But I didn't account for drawing the bogeyman's attention. He wasn't supposed to take me. He was supposed to take my *father*. To rid the world of another monster.

For months, if not years, I have heard stories about this man. Everyone has. No one knows who he is, except me.

Our first run-in was a complete accident—or maybe it was fate. At first, I didn't realize who he was. I thought he was just some rich guy going to some fancy dinner. But when I saw his phone, I knew he was a wolf in a sheep's mask.

I saw names on his phone with messages. I took a mental snapshot. But a few I already recognized … from the news of men missing and found dead.

I was suspicious, but not certain, not until the day after I ran into him. I saw the newest report of a man missing, the name I saw that Kalius had most recently messaged. As consistent as the murders were, the stories about how horrible the men had been shortly followed.

Wives, coworkers, children came forward and spoke about who these men really had been.

Monsters.

I got lucky and caught Kalius's attention. I knew he was lurking outside of my house, watching me. I could have been wrong all along, but I knew if monsters were what he was after, then I had one I was willing to serve up on a platter.

I thought he was going to kill me right away. But he didn't. Instead, he studied me and how I would react to him killing Jerry.

My plan failed, but that doesn't mean it can't evolve into something new. Maybe I can still get the bogeyman to do my bidding.

I meet his intense stare, and his hand quivers on my jaw, slipping down to my throat.

"What do you want to do about it, Elodie? Tell me."

"I don't want to talk about him right now," I say, and it's true.

A cord inside of me is drawn tight. His slightest movement plucks it like a guitar string, and I want to see how he can play me.

He smirks deviously. "Oh, yeah? What do you want to talk about then?"

"You," I whisper.

"What about me?" He releases me, crouches down, and sits on my mattress.

I want to ask him how many people he has killed.

I want to know when it started, how he honed his skills, how long he's had this creepy, custom-built kill basement, and why the hell he's obsessed with me.

I decide on a question I can't get out of my mind. "Why did you take me?"

He leans back on his hands with his ankles crossed in front of him, like this is a casual conversation he's having. Maybe I'm not the first girl he's had chained to this bed.

He looks at me and softly says, "When I target someone, I can't focus on anything else. It consumes me until I release that energy inside of me, and I do that by killing the source of my urges. For some reason, you became the subject of my latest compulsion. I might kill people, but I only rid the world of garbage, not the innocent. I protect them. Which is why you are such a mystery, Elodie."

His truthful answer takes me back a bit. But I guess if he never plans on letting me leave this room, he can say anything and everything he wants without worrying about oversharing his secrets.

"You've never used this bed to keep someone down here?" My cheeks flush, and I can't help but chuckle at the circumstance I'm in.

For God's sake, I'm blushing, asking my kidnapper about his history to ease my jealousy. I'm going insane. He smirks, and arrogance washes over his sharp features. "You are the only person I have brought down here who I have considered not killing. I put that chain in the ground just for you. I've never needed to keep someone alive and restrained before. I figured the bed would be more comfortable than the concrete."

"And the silk sheets?" I chuckle playfully, sinking further into insanity.

He shrugs. "I have good taste."

He flips over and crawls to me on the mattress. I follow his lead and lean onto my back as he moves on top of me, caging me in between his arms.

"You look better in black." His words vibrate through my body.

"Thank you," I say and wet my lips.

Blood, now dried, covers his neck, arms, chest, and abs. The blood of a man who put children through hell. My core pulses at the thought of his life being over. He deserved to die.

SILENCE AND SORROW

A thought pops into my head, a way to lengthen our time together and give me a chance to convince him not to kill me.

"Kalius?" I whisper as his head dips lower.

"Yes?" he growls as his lips graze my cheek.

"Keep me, use me, play with me, take what you want. I'm handing it over to you. I will be yours in any way you see fit. I will gain your trust, and you will gain mine." He pulls away and meets my gaze, and I will myself the courage to continue. "I want to help you take them down."

"You want to help me kill?" he asks, his voice gruff and heavy.

Nodding, I lift my hand carefully and cup his cheek, swiping my thumb across the dried blood. "Yes."

He catches me by surprise and smashes his lips on mine. His tongue plunges into my mouth, and he devours me.

A deep rumble sounds from my mouth into his, and my back arches at the mere noise. His body lowers onto mine, and he grinds his hips into me.

He releases my lips, and the look in his eyes is animalistic. "Mine to keep. Mine to use. Mine to play with."

He runs his tongue up my neck, and I gasp.

"Say it," he demands.

Panting, he wraps his strong hand around my neck and squeezes slightly.

"Yours—" I swallow and force the whispered

words through the tight opening. "Yours to keep. Yours to use. Yours to play with."

"That's right, Elodie. *Mine.*" He claims my lips once more as his fingers sweep up my side, leaving goose bumps in their wake.

The elephant in the room demands to be announced.

"I-I'm a virgin."

He drops his head against my neck, the chain jingling from the impact. "Fucking hell, Elodie. I'm going to be your first?"

I nod and bite down on my bottom lip.

"Good," he heaves. "I will be your first and your *only.* The thought of another man touching you, being inside of you … *fuck,* it makes me insane. If anyone else ever lands their hands on you, I will gut them and rip them apart."

That should definitely not turn me on. Right?

His lips latch on to my neck, and electrifying tingles I've never felt radiate from his kiss to my entire body. He licks and laps at my neck until my vision begins to spot from the pleasure.

"Get on your hands and knees," he growls, pushing my bra straps off of my shoulders and yanking my bra down, my breasts jiggling free.

He licks his lips and twirls his finger in a circle, saying, *Turn around.*

Gulping, I do as he said, rolling over onto my

hands and knees, feeling my pulse race with anticipation.

Drawing in a sharp breath, he cups my ass with his hands, squeezing tightly, catching me by surprise. I feel his warm breath for only a moment before he shoves his nose and mouth against my panties and breathes me in.

"You are pure fucking ecstasy," he groans and runs his tongue up my pussy.

I wish I could moan and show him how great that feels, how much I'm enjoying every goddamn second of this.

Shivers run down my body, and I feel him smile against my ass.

He tugs my panties aside and runs his tongue up my core. My back arches as he plunges his tongue inside of me, sucking, licking, and worshipping me.

I never knew it could be *this* amazing.

His fingers spread my cheeks, and he somehow sinks his tongue deeper.

"That's my good little pet, Elodie. You will take everything I fucking give you and thank me for it."

His words bounce against me, and I feel them in every cell of my body.

Nodding, I agree with him, although at this moment, I think I would agree to pretty much anything he said.

His finger circles my entrance as he says, "So fucking wet for me."

The tip of his finger slides inside me, pushing further and further. The feeling is alien, good, but abnormal. I've never put anything inside of me before, so this feels completely new.

As his finger slides out, pleasure pulses through me from his touch.

Holy shit, that feels so good.

He adds another finger, stretching me more and more. His fingers thrust in and out of me, and the sensations are almost overwhelming. His tongue laps at my entrance as he continues to finger-fuck me.

I've only ever had a couple of orgasms by my own hand and never by someone else. But I can feel it building inside me.

He hooks his fingers inside of me, and I drop onto my elbows, my ass staying high in the air. Oh my God, I'm so close.

He continues to pump his skillful fingers, and his other hand finds my clit, circling with a torturous rhythm.

Whispering, wishing I could scream it at the top of my lungs, I say, "Kalius, holy fuck."

He pulls his tongue away for a moment to say with his raspy and deep voice, "Say my fucking name when I make you come. I won't fucking breathe until I hear it again. Now, come for me like my good girl."

I think he was holding back before, somehow, someway, because what he's doing with his fingers and tongue right now are on a new fucking level. He groans into my pussy, and the vibrations push me over the edge.

With my face pressed sideways into the mattress, I fist the sheets and push back into his face as an explosion erupts through my body.

"Kalius!" I whisper with all of my might as my orgasm continues to tear through me.

He doesn't let up in the slightest. Instead, he slides a third finger inside of me, and I don't know how much more I can take before all the cells in my body burst from pleasure.

He removes his fingers and mouth from me, and I immediately miss their warmth and fullness. Moving my hips to the side, I watch him push his boxers down.

His full erection springs free, and the most devilish grin takes over his face.

There's no goddamn way that is going to fit.

He wraps his hand around himself, his fingers not even touching from the girth of his massive cock, and pumps himself slowly before dropping onto his knees behind me.

He slaps his dick against the top of my ass, and I sharply exhale, needing to feel him fill me up. But I'm still nervous, wondering if it's going to hurt really bad.

"Fucking hell, Elodie. I have thought about this endlessly. I can't wait to feel your little pussy stretch around me. Are you ready for this?" he asks, warming my heart by his need for consent.

"Yes," I pant and inhale, trying to prepare myself.

"Take a deep breath, baby," he instructs while spreading my legs further apart.

I do as I was told, inhaling slowly. He lines his wide tip up with my entrance, and I slowly exhale.

Gently, he pushes inside of me, and I gasp from the pressure. A sharp pinch radiates from inside of me.

"Fuuuck," he moans.

His hand reaches around my hip, finding my clit once more. The second he starts circling it, my body relaxes and begins stretching for him, taking him greedily.

He pushes further into me, continuing to rub my most sensitive spot.

"You're doing so good," he hums.

He pulls out slightly before gliding back into me, lighting up my entire body. The sensations rock through me, the pain replaced by absolute pleasure.

"There you go. Take my fucking cock," he groans.

His pace picks up, and he puts his hands on my hips, moving me against him as he thrusts.

"*Oh my God.*" The words fall from my lips without thought.

He deeply chuckles. "That's right, baby. I am your *motherfucking* god."

He pulls back and slams into me, stretching me to my limit. He wasn't giving me his full length before now, and, *fuck*, it's overwhelming.

SILENCE AND SORROW

He slams my hips against his, a loud clap of our flesh echoing into the room, over and over.

"You feel so fucking good."

He thrusts harder and faster, and my body feels like it's beginning to float with ecstasy.

"Tell me again. Tell me you're all mine," he grunts as his fingers dig sharply into my hips.

"I'm yours!" I whisper-cry as his cock plunges back inside me. "*Yours* to keep. *Yours* to use. *Yours* to play with," I recite back to him, feeling every word to my core.

"That's right. *Mine*," he rasps out.

He thrusts once more, and I fucking obliterate into a thousand pieces around him.

He relentlessly fucks me as I come, calling out, "Kalius, oh my fucking God!"

He pumps into me rapidly before groaning and pulling out of me. He spills onto me, covering my ass in his cum.

Flipping me over, he pinches my jaw and brings my lips to his, kissing me with fervor and desperation. "You are mine for-*fucking*-ever, Elodie. I'm never letting you go."

"Then, don't," I breathe into his mouth and claim his lips with mine once more.

He releases me and says, "I'll get a towel to clean you up and some new sheets."

He laughs—genuinely laughs—and I can't help

but smile back at him.

He walks across the room, ignoring the still-dead body of Jerry, and grabs a towel from a closet. He also grabs a wet wipe and begins cleaning the dried blood off of his chest, abs, neck, and arms.

His black hair falls lazily over his forehead, wet with sweat, as he walks back over to me. He is the most attractive person I've ever seen.

Gently, he cleans me up and removes the sheets. My panties are still soaked, and I think about asking for another pair.

As if he can read my mind, he says, "You can wear those for a while as a little reminder of me."

"As if being in your basement isn't enough?" I say sassily and playfully.

He smirks and walks into the room behind the mirror.

"What the fuck?!" Kalius shouts and kicks something, hearing it fly across the little room.

Looking into the mirror, I wave to try to grab his attention and hold my hands, palms up, asking what's wrong.

He storms out of the room and strides over to me. "Someone is trying to end up on my fucking table."

"What?" I ask, feeling anxious from the anger radiating off of him.

I'm not worried that he'll hit me; I'm worried about what the hell is causing him so much distress.

SILENCE AND SORROW

He flips his phone around to me and shows me
the message.

Unknown:
I know who and what you are, Kalius Noble.

"Whoever this is will lose this war. They aren't
taking away everything I have worked so hard to
build. They aren't taking you from me." He drops
his phone and cups my cheeks in his hands and rests
his forehead against mine. "I will bring this world to
fucking ruin to protect us."

Saintly Sins Duet

Book Two

Coming October 2024

Author's Note & Acknowledgments

I had the most fun bringing Kalius and Elodie to life. I hope you loved meeting them and look forward to their second novella that will be releasing next October. Kalius and Elodie hold such a special place in my heart.

Thank you dearly for picking up Silence and Sorrow. I could not live out my dream if it was not for you. I can never thank you enough.

Thank you to my best friend, who encouraged me to write Silence and Sorrow, and fell in love with their story before I even did. I would be so fucking lost without you. And my writing would be shit.

To my husband, thank you for understanding the dark side of my brain, and loving every part of me unconditionally. And for knowing and accepting that the things I had to research for this book one thousand percent put me on some kind of FBI list.

Xoxo
Bird

About the Author

Bird is a pseudonym for an author you already know and love in the romance community. Bird is her secret little dark side that she decided to finally let fly free.

You may never know who she is, but she knows who all of you are.

Behave, Little Bird.
xoxo

Made in the USA
Monee, IL
08 December 2023

47561612R00062